Thomas D. D. Dancer, Alexander Aikman, John R. Coxe

A Short Dissertation on the Jamaica Bath Waters

to which is prefixed, an introduction concerning mineral waters in general

- shewing the methods of examining them, and ascertaining their contents

Thomas D. D. Dancer, Alexander Aikman, John R. Coxe

A Short Dissertation on the Jamaica Bath Waters
to which is prefixed, an introduction concerning mineral waters in general - shewing
the methods of examining them, and ascertaining their contents

ISBN/EAN: 9783337330248

Printed in Europe, USA, Canada, Australia, Japan

Cover: Foto ©Andreas Hilbeck / pixelio.de

More available books at **www.hansebooks.com**

A SHORT

DISSERTATION

ON THE

Jamaica Bath Waters:

To which is prefixed,

A N

INTRODUCTION

CONCERNING

Mineral Waters in general;

Shewing the Methods of examining them, and ascertaining their Contents.

BY THOMAS DANCER, *M. D.*

PHYSICIAN TO THE BATH.

KINGSTON, *(JAMAICA)*

PRINTED BY D. DOUGLASS & ALEX. AIKMAN, PRINTERS TO THE KING'S MOST EXCELLENT MAJESTY.

M. DCC. LXXXIV.

TO THE

SUBSCRIBERS

AND

PATRONS

OF THIS

PUBLICATION,

The fame is refpectfully dedicated,

BY

THEIR MOST OBEDIENT HUMBLE SERVANT

THE

AUTHOR.

LIST of SUBSCRIBERS.

The following are Commiffioners to the Bath.

HIS Excellency GENERAL CAMPBELL, Governor of the Ifland of Jamaica, &c. &c. 6 copies

The Hon. Thos. Iredell, Efq. Prefident⎫
———— Rofe Herring May
———— William Patrick Brown
———— Samuel Alprefs
———— James Wildman
———— Nath. Beckford, Efq. 2 cop.
———— Robert Sewell
———— Thomas Denfon⎭ *Members of His Majefty's Privy Council.*

The Hon. S. W. Haughton, Efq. Speaker⎫
His Hon. J. Grant, Efq. Ch. juft. 2 cop.
James Rifby Whitehorne, Efq.
George C. Ricketts, Efq.
Henry Browne, Efq.
Edmund Jackfon, Efq.
Edward Eaft, Efq.⎭ *Members of the Hon. the Affembly.*

John Rodon, Efq.
Benjamin Allen, Efq.
Thomas Cockburn, Efq.
Francis Dennis, Efq.
William Elphinftone, Efq.
Jofeph Woodhoufe, Efq.
James Pinnock, Efq. 2 copies
Nathaniel Phillips, Efq. 2 do.
Thomas Chambers, Efq.
P. P. Livingfton, Efq.
William Gray, Efq.
Thomas Gray, Efq.
William Mitchell, Efq.
Richard Batty, Efq.
James Ridge, Efq.
Hugh Lewis, Efq.
William Peete, Efq.
Donald Campbell, Efq.
Sir Charles Price, Bart. 2 copies

Members of the Honorabl: the Affembly.

Sir Thomas Champneys, Bart. 2 copies
Dr. Ch. Irvine, St. Thos. in the Eaft, 2 do.
James Murray, Efq. do. 2 do.
Jofeph Orr, Efq. do. 2 do.

A.

ALLAN, John, Merchant in Kingfton
Arthur, Mr. Planter, St. James's
Ayrie, Dr. Thomas, Kingfton
Alexander, William, Efq. Meffenger of the
Hon. Houfe of Affembly

Alexander, Mr. John, Spanifh-Town
Aldred, Dr. George, Kingfton
Arthur, Mr. John Weldon, Kingfton
Allan Thomas, Merchant, Kingfton
Anderfon, Dr. James, St. Mary's
Anderfon, Mr. A. Port-Morant
Adamfon, John, Efq. Rocky-Point
Anderfon, Mr. Wm. St. Thos. in the Eaft.

B.

Baker, John Proculus, Efq.
Bruce, Stewart, Merchant, Kingfton
Ballantyne, Patrick, do. do.
Bannatyne, David, do. do.
Baird, John, do. do.
Berry, Richard, do. do.
Brooke, Dr. Rich. Spanifh-Town
Binham, Dr. George, do.
Baird, John, Efq. Kingfton   [4 cop.
Brodbelt, Frs. Rigby, M. D. Spanifh-Town
Boog, R.. Merchant, Kingfton
Bogle, R. do. do.
Bridges, Daniel, Efq. Liguanea
Brooks, Mr. G. Gen. Poft-Office
Brown, John, Merchant, Kingfton
Bell, Thomas, Efq. do. do.
Burke, Mr. St. Thos. in the Eaft,
Barret, Mr. T. do. do.
Bollington, Mr. H. do.
Brady, Mr. Francis, do.

C.

Cumine, Mr. William, Kingston
Clarke, Mr. Daniel, do.
Cuthbert, G. Esq. Provost-Marshal, 2 cop.
Cruickshank, George, Esq. Spanish-Town
Crosse, S. B. Esq. do.
Campbell, Archibald, Merchant, Kingston
Camac, Captain, St. Thomas in the East.
Clarke, Thos. M. D. Botanist to the Island
Clarke, Mr. William, Kingston
Collery, Mr. Thomas, do.
Calland, William, Merchant, do.
Campbell, John, Esq. Liguanea
Cumine, Alexander, A. M. Kingston
Clarke, James, Kingston
Carter, A. Esq. St. Thomas in the East
Clarke, Dugald, Esq. do.
Clinton, Mr. George, Port-Morant
Clinton, Mr. Abraham, do.
Clarke, Mr. William, Kingston
Clarke, Mr. William, St. Thos. in the East
Clarke, Mr. W. K. do.
Cruikshanks, Mr. W. do.
Cargill, Thomas, Esq. do.
Currie, Simon, Esq. Manchioneal
Carruthers, Dr. Joseph, St. Thos. in the East

D.

Dirom, Captain, 60th regt.
Dixon, Captain Charles, do.
Donaldson, William, Merchant, Kingston

Dilworth, William, Merchant, Kingſton
Dobbin, Clotworthy, Capt. 6oth regt.
Davis, George, Eſq. Kingſton
Donaldſon, John, Eſq. Clarendon
Davis, William, Merchant, Spaniſh-Town
Dryſdale, Dr. John, Kingſton
Dwarris, Fortunatus, M. D. do.
Davidſon, Dr. Walter, do.
Donaldſon, Robert, Eſq. Kingſton
Demetres, Mr. John, Spaniſh-Town
Davidſon, Mr. R. St. Thomas in the Eaſt
Dickſon, Mr. T. do.

E.

Eaſt, Hinton, Eſq.
Edgar, A. Eſq. St. Thomas in the Eaſt
Edgar, Mr. W. Plantain-Garden River.

F.

Farmer, Jaſper, Eſq. Kingſton
Forbes, Alexander, Merchant, do.
Fuller, Peeke, Eſq. Spaniſh-Town
Fiſher, Ralph, Merchant, Kingſton
Fullarton, Rev. Doctor
Finlayſon, David, Eſq. Weſtmoreland
Fitzſimmons, Dr. J. Naval Hoſp. Port-Royal
Flanagan, Dr. William, Kingſton
Fyfe, Dr. William, do.
Findlay, Dr. John, St. Thomas in the Eaſt
Fraſer, Mr. Alexander, do.
Fletcher, William, Dr. St. Mary's
Foulkes, Theodore, Eſq. Clarendon

G.

Grant, Dr. David, M. D. Phyfician, Kingfton
Grant, Charles, Efq. Spanifh-Town
Grant, Richard, Efq. Kingfton
Gordon, Dr. William, do.
Gibbs, Mr. W. do.
Gibbes, Mr. Walter, do.
Grant, Patrick, Efq. Clarendon.
George, Mr. T. Plantain-Garden River.
Gordon, Rob. Efq. St. Thomas in the Eaft
Graham, Mr. James, do. do.
Grant, Lachlan, Efq. do. do.
Grant, George, Efq. do. do.
Gordon, Larchin, Efq. Clarendon

H.

Hutchefon, G. R. Merchant, Kingfton
Holcombe, Thomas, do. do.
Hall, Charles, do.
Hibbert, Robert, do.
Hanbury, J. P. do.
Howard, Rev. M. M. A. St. T. in the Eaft
Henckell, John, Efq. Spanifh-Town
Henderfon, John, Efq. Salt-Ponds
Henderfon, George, Merchant, Kingfton
Hughes, ——, do. do.
Hall, Charles, Efq. Liguanea
Hughes, Mr. Edward, Kingfton
Hamilton, Alex. Efq. St. Thos. in the Eaft
Hamilton, Mr. James, do.

Hinchelwood, Mr. A. do.
Hewetfon, Dr. Wm. St. Mary's
Howel, Samuel, Efq. Spanifh-Town

I.

Jones, James, Efq. Spanifh-Town
Jackfon, John, Efq. St. James's
Jopp, Alexander, Merchant, Kingfton
Jamiefon, Robert, M. D. Phyfician, do.
Jamiefon, Dr. T. of his Majefty's fhip Janus
Jamefon, Dr. M'Millan, of the R. Artillery
Jaques, John, Efq. Kingfton
Innes, William, Efq. Manchioneal
Johnfon, Thomas Coleman, Efq. Kingfton
Irving, Mr. John
Irving, Dr. Charles, St. James's

K.

Kemys, J. Gardiner, Efq. St. Thomas in the
    Eaft, 4 copies
King, Mr. James, do.
Kelly, John, Efq. Plantain-Garden-River
Kelfall, Henry, Efq. Spanifh-Town

L.

Leflie, R. Merchant, Kingfton
Lindo, Alexander, do. do.
Lawrie, Major James, Superintendant of the
    Mufquito-Shore
Litteljohn, Alexander, Efq. Portland
Ledwich, Wm. Efq. St. Thos. in the Eaft

Lee, Dr. Thomas, Spanifh-Town
Lord, Henry, Efq. do.
Lorrain, Dr. John, do.
Langley, Thos. M. D. Phyfician, Kingfton
Leith, Dr. John, St. Mary's
Lobban, Jofeph, Efq. do.
Lithgow, ——, Efq. St. Thomas in the Eaft
Logan, Robert, Efq. do.
Lindfay, James, Efq. do.

M.

M'Murdo, William, Merchant, Kingfton
M'Neal, L. do. do.
Manby, Edward, Merchant, do.
Merchant, William, do. do.
Murray, Cornelius, do. do.
Martins, M. Efq. Spanifh-Town
Moore, John, Merchant, Kingfton
Morgan, Reverend Dr. William, do.
M'Crae, Alexander, Efq. St. Ann's
M'Kenzie, Dr. Simon, Liguanea
M'Kenzie, George, Efq. Clarendon
M'Kenzie, Dr. George, do.
M'Lean, Thomas, Efq. Spanifh-Town
M'Glafhan, Dr. Duncan, Phyfician, do.
M'Glafhan, Dr. John, Kingfton
M'Intyre, Dr. Alexander, do.
M'Leod, Alexander, Efq. Spanifh-Town
Mure, Thomas, Efq. Secretary to the Ifland
Midwinter and Trower, Drs. Kingfton
Morton, Dr. David, Kingfton

Mitchell, Dr. ——, St. Thomas in the Eaſt
M'Lean, John, Merchant, Kingſton
M'Kenzie, George, Eſq. Clarendon
M'Viccar, Dr. James, Manchioneal
M'Ewan, Dr. Wm. St. Mary's
M'Lean, Dr. Hector, do.
M' Lean, Mr. John, St. Thomas in the Eaſt
M'Pherſon, Mr. Donald, junior, do.
M'Donnel, Mr. J. do.
M'Kenzie, Mr. G. St. Thomas in the Eaſt
M'Crae, John, Eſq. St. Mary's
Mitchell, Dr. St. Thomas in the Eaſt
M'Gillivray, J. Eſq. do.
Murray, David, Eſq. do.
M'Kinlay, John, Eſq. do.
M'Pherſon, William, Eſq. do.
M'Pherſon, Donald, Eſq. do.
M'Donald, Mr. John, do.
Murray, J. Eſq. of Philiphaugh, Scotland
M'Millan, Donald, Eſq. St. Thos. in the Eaſt
M'Kenzie, Mr. J. do.
Murray, Gideon, Eſq. do.
Mickle, Dr. ——, Old-Harbour

N.

Noble, George, Merchant, Kingſton
Nembhard, Dr. George, Kingſton
Naſmyth, James, M. D. St. Mary's
Nott, Dr. Roger, Morant-Bay
Neil, Mr. Joſeph, St. Thos. in the Eaſt

O.

Organ, Dr. Patrick

P.

Pennington, Daniel, Efq. Spanifh-Town
Pinnock, Philip, Efq. do.
Porter, Dr. Robert, Kingfton
Paterfon, Robt. Efq, St Thomas in the Eaft

R.

Radcliff, Triftram, Efq. Vere
Rennals, Dr. V. Spanifh-Town, 2 copies
Redwood, Philip, Efq. Spanifh-Town
Ritchie, Alexander, Efq. Kingfton
Rowley, Admiral Jofhua, &c. &c. &c.
Robinfon, Dr. John, Kingfton, 4 copies
Rickarby, James, Merchant, do.
Reeder, John, Efq. St. Thomas in the Eaft
Rutherford, John, Merchant, Kingfton
Reid, John, Efq. Salt-Ponds
Reid, Dr. St. Mary's
Rofs, Francis, Efq. do.
Robertfon, Mr. H. St. Thomas in the Eaft
Robertfon, ——, Efq. St. David's

S.

Sheriff, T. H. Merchant, Kingfton
Simpfon, John, do. do.
Shaw,, Alexander, do. do.
Shackleford, J. E. Efq. Regifter in Chancery

Stirling, Charles, Efq. St. Ann's
Sleater, John, Efq. Kingfton
Shepherd, Dr. J. Beckett, do.
Scott, Dr. William, St. Thomas in the Eaft
Skene, James, M. D. Kingfton
Steele, Dr. Thomas, St. James's
Steele, Rev. James, Spanifh-Town
Sieben, George, Efq. Kingfton
Smith, William, Efq. do.
Spalding, Dr. Robert, Liguanea
Shaw, Mr. James
Stewart, Charles, Efq. St. Mary's
Sterling, Mr. Matt. St. Thomas in the Eaft
Sheriff, Mr. A. do.
Stodart, Dr. R. do.
Stamford, T. Efq. do.
Serjeant, Mr. R. D. do.
Smith, Mr. T. T. do.
Strahan, Mr. John, do.
Shaw, Dr. David, St. Mary's
Stout, Mr. John, Merchant, Kinfton

T.

Thomfon, Archibald, Merchant, Kingfton
Thomfon, Dr. A. Sixteen-Mile-Walk
Todd, Dr. John, Kingfton
Tyler, Elifha, Merchant, do
Trumbull, Mr. W. Port-Morant
Thom, Mr. Robert, do.
Tiernay, Dr. St. Thomas in the Eaft
Townfhend, Mr. W. do.
Taylor, Mr. D. do.

V.

Vernon, John, Efq. Kingfton

W.

Whitehorne, Sam. Efq. Spanifh-Town
Wotton, George, Efq. do.
Wynter, Thomas, Efq. do. 3 copies
White, George, Merchant, Kingfton
Woollery, Edward, Efq. Liguanea
Walker, James, M. D. Phyfician, Kingfton,
    Fellow of the Colleges of Phyficians of
    London and Edinburgh
Warren, Rev. Thomas, St. Elizabeth
Wright, Dr. William, M. D. F. R. S.
Waddell, James, Merchant, Kingfton
Wilfon, Mr. John, St. Thomas in the Eaft
Werge, Mr. T. do.

N. B. Should there be any omiffions in
the foregoing lift, Dr. *Dancer* hopes they
will be excúfed, having taken every pains to
collect the fubfcribers and to make the catalogue as complete as poffible.

PREFACE.

THE virtues of the Bath Waters have been eftablifhed by the experience of almoft a century, yet very little has been done to afcertain their particular nature. The account given by Dr. *Brown* in his hiftory of Jamaica, as well as that in the hiftory publifhed in 1774 (which are the only ones that I have ever feen) are both not only defective, but extremely erroneous. What may have been done by my predeceffors, or others, in the inveftigation of thefe waters I am totally unacquainted with, as their experiments have never come to light:

I hope therefore that my humble attempts may not be unacceptable to the public.

Although the chemical analyfis of mineral waters may not be adequate to a full explanation of their virtues and effects, yet it certainly tends to throw confiderable light on their operation, and to direct to a more fafe, certain, and beneficial application of them. It is even ufeful to know what a mineral water does *not* contain, as will be feen from the miftaken notions that have been entertained concerning the waters here treated of.

To make the fubject univerfally intelligible, I have, in an introductory part, given a few chemical fketches relating to it; in which I can pretend to no novelty or merit, unlefs from the mode of arrangement, and from having avoided, as much as poffible, technical obfcurity.

I might have enlarged much more than I have done upon the ufes of the Bath waters, but it would have been impoffible to particularife dif- eafes and fymptoms with fo much nicety, as to preclude the neceffity of advice, or make a book ferve the place of a phyfician; but I prefume I have faid enough to fhew their extenfive utility, and to explain in fome degree their nature and operation. Could I have told how to make the publica- tion more ufeful, and more deferving of the liberal patronage it has met with, no pains fhould have been wanting; but having done my beft, I have only to add my grateful ac- knowledgments, and to pray that the moft favourable conftruction may be put on my endeavours.

CONTENTS.

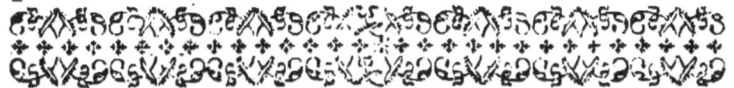

INTRODUCTION;

CONTAINING

A fhort Effay on Mineral Waters.

SECTION I.

MINERAL WATERS conftituting a very ufeful branch of the Materia Medica, have from the earlieft ages engaged the attention of mankind: As they are various in their nature they afford a remedy for various diforders, but are particularly beneficial in complaints of the chronical kind, where all other medicines frequently fail. The improvements which have been

lately made in chemiftry have enabled phyficians fo fully to explore and afcertain the
nature of many of the mineral waters, as to
imitate them with great exactitude ; and, as
fome of them owe their efficacy to a volatile
principle that fuddenly efcapes notwithftanding every means that can be made ufe of to
detain it, the * artificial impregnations of .
waters may in a few inftances be preferable
to thofe formed by nature; that is, when they
cannot be ufed on the fpot, or where they cannot be obtained in a perfect ftate, *viz.* without
having previoufly fuffered fome change, if
not lofs of their properties : But, in general,
nature prepares this clafs of remedies much
more perfectly in her laboratory than the
chemift can do in his ; for though we may
by analyfis detect the feveral principles of a
mineral water, yet we cannot always again

---

* Should any of my readers be defirous of being inftructed in
the method of preparing the mineral waters artificially, I muft
beg leave to refer them to Dr. *Prieftly*, or to a late pamphlet by
Dr. *Elliot*, in which is explained the particular manner of imita-
ting almoft all the moft ufeful mineral waters, whether faline,
chalybeate, or fulphureous.——The apparatus for this purpofe,
as invented by Dr. *Prieftly*, and improved by Dr. *Naoth* and others,
may be bought of the different druggifts in this ifland.

combine thofe principles in the mode they before exifted, and fo as to give them the fame properties. Mineral waters will therefore ever retain their importance; and as they are, in fome difeafes of the human body, the moft efficacious kind of remedy, fo they are at the fame time the moft agreeable one, and can with lefs inconveniency or difguft be perfifted in, for a due length of time, than any other whatfoever.

Among the great number of mineral waters found in different parts of the world, I may with great fafety affert, that there cannot be a more valuable one than that which is the fubject of this publication, or that poffeffes greater virtues in the cure of fundry difeafes; to make the nature and effects of which better underftood, it will be neceffary to premife fomething concerning *mineral waters in general*, and of the methods made ufe of in examining them: I hope to explain the fubject fo as to render it intelligible to thofe who have never before ftudied it, and have no previous acquaintance with chemiftry; in order to which, we muft take a flight * furvey of chemical bodies, and of their feveral affinities or relations to each other.

A General View of Chemical Bodies.

ALL the bodies in nature, confidered in relation to their chemical properties, are divifible into fix claffes, *viz.*—1. Salts, — 2. Inflammable Subftances, — 3. Earths and earthy Subftances,—4. Metals and metallic Subftances,—5. Water,—6. Air and aerial Subftances.

I. S A L T S.

THESE are defined by Chemifts *to be fufible with heat, fapid in the mouth, and foluble in water;* but the two laft mentioned pro-

---

* The fcience of chemiftry has fuch an extenfive connection with the arts, and with the other branches of natural knowledge, that I flatter myfelf the following outlines may be ufeful not merely in relation to mineral waters, but to many other fubjects that require inveftigation—as, the procefs of fugar boiling, diftillation of rum, manufacture of indigo, manufacture of pot-afh, &c. &c. all which depend directly on chemiftry, and certainly require fome fhare of chemical knowledge.

perties, conftitute their moft general charac‑
ter. It is not neceffary in fuch a fketch as
this to ftudy much precifion; I hope there‑
fore the chemifts will not complain of my
definitions being inaccurate and incomplete.

The following table exhibits a general
view of falts, and requires only a fimple in‑
fpection to be perfectly underftood.

TABLE OF SALTS.

I. SIMPLE.

1. Acid.	Foffile.	Vitriolic, *viz.*	*Oil of Vitriol*
		Nitrous, —	*Aqua Fortis*
		Muriatic, —	*Spirit of Salt*
	Vegetable.	Acetous, *viz.*	*Vinegar*
		Tartarous, —	*Tartar*
2. Alkali.	Fixed.	Vegetable, *viz. Pearl Afhes*	
		mild *or Salt of Tartar*	
		cauftic	
		Foffile, — *Barilla*	
	Volatile.	Volatile, *viz. Sp. of Hartfhorn*	
		mild *or Sal. Volatile*	
		cauftic	

II. COMPOUND.

1. Neutral, compofed of *Acid* and *Alkali*.
2. Earthy, compofed of *Acids* and *Earths*.
3. Metallic, compofed of *Acids* and *Metals*.

The above view of the fimple falts, I think, can require no fort of explanation; it is obvious from the arrangement, that they are generically diftinguifhed by being either acid or alkaline; the acid falts are either *foffile*, or *vegetable:* Again, the foffile acids are of three kinds, *vitriolic*, *nitrous*, and *muriatic*; the common names of which are fubjoined. The vitriolic acid is the fame thing as *oil of vitriol*; the nitrous acid is *aqua fortis*, or *fpirits of nitre*; and the muriatic acid is *fpirit of falt*. In the fame manner the alkaline falts are divided and fubdivided. By arranging fubftances in this method, the memory is much affifted, and defcriptions rendered unneceffary. I fhall proceed to enumerate the other compound falts in the fame manner.

I. NEUTRAL SALTS.

ARE thofe which are formed by the union of an acid and alkali; having the properties of neither, but making (as chemifts fpeak) a *tertium quid*; that is, a new fubftance *fui generis*, or of a diftinct kind.

The following table exhibits a catalogue of moſt of the neutral ſalts, and ſhews the manner in which they are formed. It is to be thus underſtood; *viz.* the *vitriolic* acid in the firſt column, combined with the *vegetable* alkali in the ſecond, makes the neutral ſalt, in the third column, called *vitriolated tartar:*—Again, the *vitriolic* acid, with the *foſſile alkali* in the next line, forms *Glauber's ſalt*, &c. &c.

TABLE OF NEUTRAL SALTS.

ACID.	ALKALI.	NEUTRAL SALTS.
1. *Vitriolic.*	Vegetable,	*Vitriolated Tartar*
	Foſſile,	*Glauber's Salts*
	Volatile,	*Vitriolic Ammoniac*
2. *Nitrons.*	Vegetable,	*Nitre, or Salt-petre*
	Foſſile,	*Cubic Nitre*
	Volatile,	*Nitrous Ammcniac*
3. *Muriatic.*	Vegetable,	*Digeſtive Salt*
	Foſſile,	*Common Salt*
	Volatile,	*Crude Ammoniac*
4. *Vegetable.*	Vegetable,	*Diuretic Salt*
	Foſſile,	*Rochelle, or Seignette do.*
	Volatile,	*Spirits of Mindererus*

Table of such Earthy and Metallic salts as are found in Mineral Waters:

I. WITH THE VITRIOLIC ACID, AND

1. *Earths.*

Calcareous earth, } Selenites, or Gypsum

Magnesia, } Epsom Salts, or bitter purging do.

Clay or particular earth, - *Allum*

2. *Metals*

Zinc, - *White Vitriol*

Iron, - *Green Vitriol*

Copper, - *Blue Vitriol*

II. WITH THE NITROUS ACID, AND

Calcareous earth, - Calcareous nitre. *(doubtful)*

III. WITH THE MURIATIC ACID, AND

Calcareous earth,
Magnesia, } Fixed ammoniac.

I have judged it needless in this place to enumerate any of the metallic salts, except such as are found in waters, and of which it was proper to know the compofition. The next general clafs, is that of

II. INFLAMMABLE SUBSTANCES.

THESE are such bodies as (without any definition) are known to take flame and confume with heat. Under this head are included all oils, refins, fulphur, ardent fpirits, &c.

The inflammability of bodies depends on a principle they contain called by chemifts phlogifton; which principle exifts in all bodies, but in different quantities and in different ftates of combination; whence their difference in refpect of inflammability and various other properties. So many phenomena in nature depend on this pervading principle, that the ftudy of it conftitutes a main branch of chemical philofophy. We fhall fee hereafter what connection it has with the fubject of mineral waters, but at prefent we need take no further notice of it.

III. METALLIC BODIES.

THE well known properties of thefe are their great fpecific gravity and fufibility with certain degrees of heat. All the metals contain a great portion of phlogifton; deprived of which they lofe their metallic form, and are reduced to a fort of earth called calx,— thus e. g. cerufle is the calx of lead.

C

The metals, in their foffile ftate, are found in various forms :

1. Virgin or pure.
2. In ores combined with earths.
3. Mineralized with fulphur and arfenic
4. Diffolved by acids or by other means, and mixed with mineral waters.

TABLE OF EARTHS.

I. ABSORBENTS.

The character of thefe is their effervefcence with acids : they are of two kinds:

1. Calcareous, *viz.* chalk, &c. which convert by heat into quick-lime, and become cauftic. This is effected by the expulfion of fixed air; which as foon as they imbibe again they lofe their caufticity and become mild.

2. Magnefia, which does not convert into quick-lime, or become cauftic as the preceding.

II. CHRYSTALLINE or FLINTY.

Thefe are hard and ftrike fire with fteel : are either

1. Apyrous, *i. e.* indeftructible by heat as fome of the precious ftones, or

2. Vitrefcent or fufible, running by heat into glafs; fuch are common flints, fand, &c.

III. ARGILLACEOUS,

Or Clays, which do not effervefce with acids, nor melt into glafs, but are unchangeable in the fire.

IV. MICACEOUS.

Stones of a fhining laminated or fibrous texture. They do not effervefce with acids, nor ftrike fire with fteel, but are either

1. Talcky, which in a ftrong heat are vitrefcent, or

2. Afbeftos, Amianthos, &c. indeftructible by heat.

N. B. Gypfum and gypfeous matters, which are fometimes confidered under the head of earths, are more properly earthy falts. *(Vid. table of earthy falts)*

Spars are ftones of very different natures, and arrange under abforbent earths, micaceous earths, &c.

Marles are abforbent earths.

V. WATER.

THE properties of water are too well known to require any defcription. Pure elementary water is hardly to be obtained, but it may be confidered either as fuch, or elfe impregnated with foreign matters, as, particularly, in mineral waters.

VI. AERIAL MATTERS.

AIR, as well as water, has by all philofophers been confidered as an elementary fubftance; but this feems to be brought into fome doubt by the late celebrated experimenters in chemiftry, who have difcovered many *fpecies* of air, and diftinguifh that by which animal life is fupported, as *atmofphe*.

ric or refpirable air : The other kinds more particularly deferving of note are,

1. Fixed or mephitic air +.
2. Phlogifticated air, which is either
    1. Inflammable, taking fire, or
    2. Non - inflammable, extinguifhing flame.

Thefe kinds of air are varioufly produced, and exhibit wonderful phenomena; but this is not a place to enter into any further confideration of that curious fubject. *

Having now pointed out the general and diftinguifhing characters of the feveral claffes of chemical bodies, I fhall proceed to explain the *affinities* of thefe, or the relations which they have to each other; upon which depend all the proceffes in chemiftry, as well as many of the moft important operations in nature.

---

† Mephitic Air is demonftrated to be an Acid.
(Vid. BEWLEY apud PRIESTLY.)
* Vid. PRIESTLY and others.

On *Chemical Affinities*.

THE affinities of bodies fignify their difpofition to unite, or the attraction they have for each other, which is owing to fome unknown relation between them : this attraction is greater between fome than others, and is therefore called *elective* : — For example, acids have an attraction both for *alkalies* and abforbent earths, but a much ftronger attraction for the former than the latter ; in confequence of which, if an abforbent earth be firft diffolved in an acid, and afterwards an alkali be added, the acid having a greater affinity to the latter will unite with it and depofit the earth. Again, acids in general have a greater attraction for earths than for metals, fo that if you add an earth to the folution of a metal in any acid, the metal will be precipitated, It is in this way that various combinations and decompofitions are effected, and that we are enabled to analyze bodies and detect their principles. I need not here give any further illuftration of the fubject, as the application of it to the inveftigation of mineral waters, which this is intended to explain, will exhibit a perfect view of it. All that is further required in this place, is, to point out the known laws of affinities, as they have been difcovered in the courfe of experiment and in the practice of chemiftry : thefe have been reduced into tables : the following one is the moft approved, as being corrected by fome of the greateft philofophers of the age.

The table is thus to be underftood, *viz.* Under the head of acids is placed, firft, phlogifton, then alkali mild, &c. the meaning of which is, that acids have an attraction for thofe different fubftances according to the order in which they are placed, *i. e.* they have a greater attraction for phlogifton than alkalies, for alkalies than abforbents, earths, &c.

Table of Affinities or Elective Attractions.

I. ACIDS IN GENERAL.

1. Phlogifton	3. Quick-lime, or *cauftic*
2. Fixed alkali;	*calcareous earth*
cauftic mild	4. Magnefia

5. Calcareous earth *mild*
6. Volatile alkali *cauſtic*
7. Metallic ſubſtances *in general*

8. Volatile alkali *mild*
9. Earth of alum
10. Pure or precious metals.

2. VITRIOLIC ACID.

Vid. acids in general.
1. Zinc
2. Nickell
3. Cobalt
4. Iron
5. Copper

6. Silver
7. Tin
8. Lead and Mercury
9. Volatile Alkali
10. Earth of Alum.

3. NITROUS ACID.

Vid. acids in gen.
1. Zinc
2. Lead or Tin
3. Iron
4. Biſmuth and An-
timony

5. Copper
6. Arſenic
7. Mercury
8. Silver
9. Platina.

4. MURIATIC ACID.

Vid. acids in gen.
1. Zinc
2. Iron
3. Tin
4. Regulus of Antim.

5. Copper
6. Lead
7. Silver
8. Mercury
9. Gold.

5. VEGETABLE ACID.

1. Iron

2. Copper.

6. MEPHITIC AIR, or MEPHITIC ACID.

Metallic fubftances   Fixed alkali
Cauftic calcar. earth   Earth of Magnefia
   or quick-lime   Volatile Alkali

7. ALKALIES IN GENERAL.

Vitriolic acid   Vegetable acid
Nitrous acid   Oils. Phlogifton, or
Muriatic acid   Sulphur

8. CALCAREOUS EARTHS.

Vitriolic acid   Muriatic acid
Nitrous acid   Sulphur

9. PHLOGISTON.

Nitrous acid   Metallic bodies
Vitriolic acid   Alkalies
Muriatic acid

10. SULPHUR.

Fixed alkali   Silver
Quick-lime   Antimony
Iron   Mercury
Copper   Arfenic
Lead   Volatile alkali
Tin

11. METALLIC SUBSTANCES in general.

Muriatic acid   Phlogifton
Vitriolic acid   Fixed air
Nitrous acid

D

12. GOLD,————Aqua regia

13. SILVER.

Muriatic acid   Nitrous acid
Vitriolic acid   Lead, Copper

14. MERCURY.

Muriatic acid   Gold
Vitriolic acid   Silver
Nitrous acid   Lead, &c.

15. IRON.

Vitriolic acid   Nitrous acid
Muriatic acid   Regulus of antimony

16. COPPER.

Vitriolic acid   Nitrous acid
Muriatic acid   Vegetable acid

I flatter myfelf that the preceding fketches
are fufficiently intelligible to every reader
who may think it worth his pains to give
the flighteft attention to them; and that
they will ferve to render what follows on
Mineral Waters eafily comprehended.

CHAPTER II.

On the CONTENTS of MINERAL WATERS.

AS this is not a work intended for the
perufal of the learned, I do not think
it requifite to enter largely into the inveftigation of the fubject, but fhall content myfelf, according to the plan I fet off with, in
giving a plain and eafy introduction to it.
Such of my readers as may be induced to
ftudy it more fully, and to extend their refearches into this pleafing and ufeful fcience,
muft have recourfe to other authors; amongft
whom I would particularly recommend Dr.
Faulkener, one that in this part of my work
I am particularly indebted to.

The lift of matters contained in mineral
waters was formerly much larger than at
prefent, later experience having demonftrated the impoffibility of many impregnations
fuppofed by the old chemifts, particularly
the nitrous and ammoniacal falts, of which
we find fo frequent mention in former wri-
ters : The acids of thefe falts have never
(like the vitriolic) been found feparate, and

if they were, they would still want a proper
base, as neither the vegetable or volatile alkali
have ever been discovered in a fossile state.

TABLE exhibiting the several CONTENTS of
MINERAL WATERS.

I. *SALTS.*

1. Acid,   - *Vitriolic in a separate state.*
2. Alkali,   - *Fossile Alkali.*
3. Neutral, - *Glauber's Salt, Common do.*

II. *INFLAMMABLES.*

1. FOSSILE OIL, *viz.* PETROLEUM.

1. Separate, or float-ing on the surface of waters.	2. Combined with an *Alkali* in form of a *Soap.*

2. SULPHUR.

1. *Per se,* diffused or suspended.	3. Combined with Calcareous Earth in a caustic state, forming *Calcareous Hepar Sulphuris.*
2. Combined with *Alkali,* forming *Hepar Sulphuris.*	

III. *EARTHS and EARTHY SALTS.*

1. CALCAREOUS EARTH.

1. In a *caustic* state, or deprived of fix-	ed Air. 2. Combined with

the Vitriolic Acid,   Sulphur, forming
forming Selenites.   Hepar Sulphuris.
3. Combined with

2. EARTH OF MAGNESIA *diſſolved.*

1. By Vitriolic Acid,   2. By Muriatic Acid,
forming   *Epſom*   conſtituting a *Salt*
Salts.   that has no name.

3. EARTH OF ALLUM.

Forming with Vitriolic Acid the Salt of Alum

IV. *METALLIC MATTERS.*

1. COPPER *diſſolved.*

By the Vitriolic Acid   Blue Vitriol.
in the form of

2. IRON *diſſolved.*

1. By Fixed Air.   form of *Green Vit.*
2. Vitriolic Acid in   3. *Hepar Sulphuris.*

3. ZINC *diſſolved.*

Vitriolic Acid, in form of *White Vitriol.*

V. *AERIAL MATTERS.*

1. Common, or *at-*   *ed* Air.
moſpheric Air,   3. Phlogiſticated, or
2. Mephitic, or *fix-*   *inflammable* Air.

The above table comprehends, on the authority of the beſt Chemiſts, all the known impregnations of mineral waters. Many other matters, as I have ſaid, were formerly included ; but I ſuggeſted the reaſon why in particular the nitrous and ammoniacal ſalts cannot have an exiſtence in mineral waters. For ſimilar reaſons none of the metals, except Iron, Copper, and Zinc, are ever found in waters, *viz.* becauſe there are no foſſile menſtrua capable of diſſolving them, the vitriolic acid and hepar ſulphuris not acting on the other metals except by the aſſiſtance of heat, or under ſome other circumſtances that are not ſuppoſed to take place in the bowels of the earth.

Arſenic has however, in particular, been conjectured to be preſent in ſome waters ; but in the opinion of the beſt authors, this poiſonous ſemi-metal is only ſoluble in water when deprived of its phlogiſton or ſulphur, in which ſtate it cannot be-found in ores.

The exiftence of an * actual Sulphur in waters has been long queftioned, but it feems on very good evidence, as we fhall fee when we come to the manner of analyfing waters, to be really found in fome few of them. The aerial impregnations of waters are of late dif-covery, and have thrown an entire new light upon the fubject, as they account for feveral combinations among the fixed matters, as well as for the medicinal efficacy of many of the waters of principal note.

I fhall here fubjoin a catalogue of the moft important mineral fprings in the various parts of the globe, with a fummary of their con-tents, according to the lateft and moft ap-proved analyfis; which may ferve not only to gratify curiofity, but to convey a general idea of their medicinal qualities and ufes in the cure of difeafes.

---

* Some chemifts have fuppofed the Sulphur found in mineral waters did not exift in the waters as a fulphur, but is formed af-terwards by a new union of the component principles.

CATALOGUE OF THE MOST CELEBRATED
MINERAL WATERS.

Aix-la-Chapelle.—Thofe Waters contain an
actual Sulphur, and are very hot.

Bath (Englifh) Waters.—Contain fixed Air,
phlogifticated Air, Hepar Sulphuris with
Quick-lime, and a little Iron —
Vid. Faulkener, Nooth, Priefly.

Bath (Jamaica)   *Vid. Analyfis following.*

Bareges.— Hepar Sulphuris, Bitumen, and
Sea Salt.

Buxton.—Similar to *Brifol.*

Brifol.—Calcareous Earth, marine Salt, and
fome Sulphur.   *Vid. Elliott.*

Caroline Baths (in Germany).—Pure alkaline
Salt, calcareous Earth, and a little Iron.
Vid. Hoffman.

Cheltenham. — Epfom, or bitter purging
Salts.   *Vid. Lewis.*

Hartfell.—Martial or green Vitriol in confiderable quantity.   *Lewis.*

Iflington.—A Chalybeate Water.

Moffat (in Scotland). — Sulphur and marine Salt.   *Plummer.*

Moffat (in Jamaica).—The fame as the a-
bove.

Vid. Analyfis by Dr. Mitchell.

Pyrmont.—A great deal of fixed Air, by
which Iron is diffolved in it. *Brownrigg.*

Spa.—Fixed Air, Ocher, Sulphur.

Sedlitz (in Bohemia).—Epfom or purging
Salts.

Teplitz (in Germany).—Is a Spring of pure
hot Water.   *Hoffman.*

Tilbury.—Alkaline Salt.   *Lewis.*

Wicklow (in Ireland).—Copper, or blue
Vitriol.

Smith's (in Jamaica).—A martial Vitriol,
like the *Hartfell Spa.* Dr. Clarke found
that it is alfo impregnated with fixed
Air, and fufpects the Iron to be kept diffolved by this as well as the Acid.

E.

Comparative View of the Temperature of the several Hot Springs in different Parts of the World.

		Farenheit.
Aix la Chapelle,		
	Bain de l'Empereur,	127
	Bain des Pauvres,	112
Briſtol Hot-well — —		76
Buxton, — — — —		59
Mallow, — — —		63
Bath (in England.)	Croſs Bath —	112
	King's do. —	116
	Hot do. —	116
	Hot Spring —	116
Bareges, higheſt, — —		112
—— *(Jamaica)* — —		126
Dax (in Guienne), ſaid to be —		140

Japan Hot Waters, ſaid to be near the boiling point.

* *Muſq. Sh.* Waters, near the boiling point.

---

* I am informed by my friend *Major Lawrie,* Superintendent of the Muſquito-ſhore, (a Gentleman well known for his active ſervices in the defence of that valuable country, where he reſided many years, and employed a very attentive obſervation on every uſeful and curious object,) that ſo great is the heat of this ſpring that either animal or vegetable ſubſtances, placed in the reſervoir into which it runs, are in a moderate ſpace of time rendered fit for uſe, and that the Indians accordingly frequently dreſs their food in it. It appears neverthelefs to contain no mineral impregnation.

Of the Method of Analyfing Mineral Waters.

IT has been before remarked, that there is no water to be obtained perfectly pure. That which is moft free from impurities is fnow water, next rain water *, and then the waters of limpid rivers; but they all contain more or lefs of earthy and faline matter, even after repeated diftillations, which has favoured the hypothefis of the ancient philofopher, that earth and all things were formed of water.

The firft thing to be attended to in the examination of any water is not its pellucidity, or apparent purity, but its weight, the pureft water being always the lighteft. The gravity of water is afcertained either by weighing a certain meafure of it in a well adjufted pair of fcales, or by the water poife called the hydrometer. Where proper fcales

† A fufpicion has been entertained, that the rain water of this country contained vitriolic acid; to determine this I collected fome in a glafs veffel during a heavy fhower, which I tried with the folutions of filver, lead, and mercury in the nitrous acid;— With the firft, there appeared a light purple tinge, which at length became reddifh; with the lead it dropped a white precipitate, and the fame with mercury, which I allowed to remain for 24 hours, without obferving any change to yellow, as fhould have happened had there been any vitriolic acid prefent.—*Vid. page* 16.J

and weights, or the above inftrument cannot be procured, another method has been
propofed for comparing the relative weight
of the water of any mineral fpring with the
other waters in the neighbourhood, *viz.* by
tincturing the water with faffron, or any
other colouring matter that makes but little
addition to its own weight, and then infert-
ing the bottle filled with it in a veffel of the
water you want to compare it with. If the
coloured water is fpecifically heavier than
the common water, it will of courfe run out
and communicate a tincture to the water in
which the bottle is immerfed.

Table of the Weights of different Waters.

		Oz.	Dr.	Gr.
Of diftilled water,	1 pint weighs	15	1	50
Rain water,	ditto	15	2	40
Spring water,	ditto	15	3	129
Sea water,	ditto	15	5	20

After having afcertained the apparent and
fenfible qualities of any water with its relative weight to other water, or to pure water, we may proceed to try it by fome of
the moft ordinary and general methods, as
follow :

1. If it lathers well with Soap.
2. If it curdles milk.
3. If it effervefces on the addition of acid or alkali.
4. If it changes the colours of blue flowers, infufed in it for fome time, either to red or green.
5. If it turns milky on adding to it a few drops of any of the following folutions, *viz.*

    1. A folution of hepar fulphuris *(i. e. liver of fulphur,)* in water.
    2. A folution of faccharum faturni, *(i. e. fugar of lead,)* in diftilled water.
    3. A folution of lead in aqua fortis.
    4. A folution of filver in ditto.

Or, laftly, if it ftrikes a black or purple colour with the powder or tincture of Galls.

By thefe general trials we can difcover not only the degree of purity in a water, but if it contains any mineral impregnation we can form fome probable conjecture as to the nature thereof, to direct us in our further refearches. The explanation of the above

modes of trial will be feen prefently as we
go on to point out more particularly how
the various fubftances contained in mineral
waters may be feverally detected.

*I. To difcover the Aerial Impregnations of
Waters.*

I. FIXED AIR,—firft, gives to waters a
fparkling appearance and poignant tafte, fi-
milar to Champaigne or Perry, which li-
quors, as well as many others, contain a
confiderable quantity of it *.

Secondly, Waters containing fixed air added to lime water precipitates the calcareous
earth which was only rendered foluble in
water by being deprived of its fixed air.

Thirdly, Waters containing fixed air have
the fingular property of diffolving iron.

---

* Waters containing fixed air are difficultly kept, the bottles
burfting ; Mr. SHACKLEFORD lately returned from the continent
of North America, informs me, that, at the famed plains of Sa-
ratoga, he faw, in company with his fellow traveller Dr. JAMES,
(a gentleman well known for his medical abilities) a mineral water that contained fo much elaftic air, that bottles only about
half filled were broke by it.

II. INFLAMMABLE AIR in waters, as alfo fixed air, may be collected, by tying an oiled bladder over the neck of a bottle containing the water. Inflammable air is lighter than common air, has a peculiar fmell, and takes flame * when it approaches any burning body.

A more accurate method of trial may be feen in the works of that learned philofopher Dr. *Prieftly,* to whom I muft refer my readers for more ample inftruction refpecting this and the feveral other fpecies of phlogifticated air.

To difcover an acid in Waters.

THE only acid found in waters in a feparate ftate *(vid. table,)* is the vitriolic, and moft commonly that fpecies of it called the *volatile fulphureous,* from the fmell, &c. which it has from the phlogifton with which it is combined.

In whatever form the vitriolic acid enters

---

* The damps of mines are either fixed or inflammable air.

into waters, it may be detected in the following manner :

1. By the infusion of blue flowers in the
water, which, if there be an acid, will become *red* *.

This laft, though a common one, is by
itfelf not decifive, becaufe fixed air and alum
in waters will effect the fame change.

2. By adding to the water a little alkaline
falt, or a few drops of oil of Tartar.

If the acid be prefent in any quantity, it
will excite an effervefcence with the alkali.

3. By dropping into the water a tincture
of foap in ardent fpirits, provided the water
contains an acid it will unite immediately
with the alkali of the foap, and the oil,
which is the other ingredient in the compofition of foap, is feparated and renders the
water milky : This ferves to explain the effect of hard waters in general in curdling
foap.

---

* Alkalies turn blue vegetables of a *green* colour, *(vid. p.* 17.)

4. By dropping into the water, a folution of hepar fulphuris, which is a combination of fulphur and alkali : The fame attraction, where there is an acid, takes place here as above in No. 3; the acid unites with the alkali, and the fulphur precipitated makes the water turbid and milky.

I obferved that an aluminous impregnation gives to waters tried in the above manner moft of the fame appearances as the vitriolic acid in a feparate ftate ; but to diftinguifh aluminous water from thofe containing an acid, we may,

1. Repeat the above experiment on the waters after they have ftood for fome time; if the changes produced were caufed by an alum in them, the fame refult will follow on making the fame trials; but the acid of waters being, as was before faid, generally the volatile vitriolic, this upon the water ftanding for fome time flies off.

2. Waters containing an acid will effervefce with and diffolve magnefia, remaining

E

perfectly clear, (provided only the neceffary quantity of magnefia is made ufe of,) but when they contain an alum, the addition of magnefia will caufe a precipitation, the vitriolic acid having a greater attraction for that than the aluminous earth.

There remains one more teft, which ferves to difcover the vitriolic acid either in a feparate or combined ftate; this is an *unfaturated* * folution of lead in the *nitrous* acid, which being added to any water that containc the vitriolic acid, this acid *(viz. the vitriolic)* having a greater attraction for lead than the nitrous, *(vid. table of affinities,)* unites with the lead in place of the latter, and the fubftance formed by this union, called a *plumbum corneum*, being not foluble in water, difturbs the tranfparency of it. It is requifite in the above experiment that there fhould be a redundancy of acid in the teft, to prevent the lead from being precipitated by any calcareous earth the water may at the fame time contain.

---

* *Unfaturated*, fignifies, not fo much as the acid is capable of diffolving.

To difcover an Alkali in Waters.

THE alkali found in mineral waters we have faid is always the foffile, the vegetable being generated only on the furface of the earth.

An alkali in waters is difcovered,

1. By their turning the blue flowers to a *green* colour.

2. By their effervefcing on the addition of an acid.

3. By their precipitating chalk from its folution in aqua fortis.

N. B. The aqua fortis fhould be faturated with the chalk, (*i. e.* contain as much as it is capable of diffolving,) or elfe the part of the acid that remains unfaturated will diffolve the alkali in the water fo that it will not precipitate the chalk.

4. By their precipitating an ochre from folutions of iron in the vitriolic acid, or from a folution of green vitriol in water, the acid of the vitriol having a greater attraction for the alkali than the metal, *(vid. table of affinities.)*

As the prefence of a *volatile* alkali in waters is not admitted, it is needlefs to adduce any of the criteria. I fhall however, for form's fake, obferve, that,

1. A folution of corrofive fublimate in diftilled water is precipitated by the *volatile* alkali in a *white*, but by the fixed alkali in a *red* or *brown* powder.

2. If a water contains any quantity of volatile alkali, it will acquire, from copper immerfed in it, a fine blue tincture.

To difcover the Neutral Salts in Mineral Waters.

I. GLAUBER'S SALT.

THIS falt is known,

1. By its tafte and the form of its chryftals, which are hexagonal: thefe may be eafily obtained from waters containing it by a flow evaporation till a pellicle forms on the furface, and then placing the liquor at reft for the chryftals to fhoot: the addition of a little fpirit of wine towards the end affifts the chryftallization.

2. By the folution of the falt in water coagulating when fpirit of wine is added to

it ; the fpirits attracting a part of the moif-
ture from the falt, it begins to refume its
chryftalline form.

3. By its fufibility in a gentle heat, which
is a property peculiar to this neutral falt.

4. By no precipitation taking place on adding an alkali to it when diffolved in water,
which always happens to falts with an earthy
bafe, as Epfom falt, &c. *(vid. table of affinities.)*

5. By the precipitation of a yellow powder *(i. e.* a turbith mineral) on adding a folution of mercury in the nitrous acid, the
mercury leaving the nitrous acid to unite
with the vitriolic.

II. COMMON SALT, is known,

1. By the figure of its chryftals, which
are cubes, and which may be obtained by
long boiling, and then placing the liquor to
cool.

2. By its decrepitation *(crackling)* on
being placed on a hot iron.

3. By its decompofition and fuffocating
fumes, on adding either the vitriolic or the
nitrous acid, which have a greater attraction
for the alkaline bafe than the muriatic acid,
of which it is formed, *(vid. affinities.)*

4. Waters containing fea falt, or the muriatic acid, precipitate lead and filver from
aqua fortis, the muriatic acid having a greater
attraction for thofe metals than the nitrous.

5. The refiduum of waters containing fea
falt, added to aqua fortis, conftitute an aqua
regia capable of diffolving gold: It may be
tried with gold leaf, or a mark on the touch-
ftone.

Although the prefence of the other neutral falts in mineral waters be fo very doubtful, I fhall neverthelefs point out the cha-
racteriftic properties by which they may be
diftinguifhed.

1. *Nitre* is known, 1ft, by the peculiar
form of its chryftals,—2d, by its deflagration
or manner of burning,—3d, by its turning
the flefh of animals red.

.2. *Calcareous nitre,* or nitre compoſed of an earthy baſe, does not deflagrate as common nitre, but bliſters, and being ſubjected to a ſtrong heat, the acid is expelled and the earth converted into quick-lime.—A ſolution of calcareous nitre is alſo expoſed by the addition of alkali.

3. *Common ammoniac* may be known by its giving out the volatile alkali on adding a fixed one, the acid having a greater affinity for the latter : the volatile alkali is immediately perceived by its pungent vapours when applied to the noſtrils.

To diſcover Sulphur in Waters.

FEW of the waters which, from their ſmell and other properties, have been called ſulphureous, contain a *real* or *actual* ſulphur, but either a hepar ſulphuris, or elſe a ſulphureous Gas, *(i. e.* the phlogiſton) in ſome mode of combination hitherto not very well underſtood.

Waters that contain an actual ſulphur, as it is only ſuſpended, not diſſolved, generally depoſit it about the ſides of the veſſels or reſervoirs in which they are placed; but when preſent only in a ſmall quantity, ſo as not to be perceptible in the foregoing manner, the ſand or mud of the ſprings may be dried and thrown on a plate of hot iron ; if there be any ſulphur contained therein the fumes will preſently diſcover it.

Waters containing a *hepar ſulphuris*, or ſulphur united with an alkali, (in which form it is rendered ſoluble in water,) are diſtinguiſhed,

1. By their fœtid ſmell, which reſembles that of the ſcourings of a foul gun.

2. By their tarniſhing the white metals, as ſilver, of a purple or black colour, and gold, of a deep yellow or copper colour.

3. By their lacteſcence on the addition of acids, which by attracting the alkali precipitate the ſulphur.

4. By their turning a ſolution of ſugar of lead of a brown colour, and by their vapours rendering viſible characters wrote with the

above folution, which is the common fym-. pathetic ink. The phlogifton which thefe vapours contain partly revive the metal in the faccharum faturni, and thus make the cha-racters vifible.

Sulphur diffolved in water by means of calcareous earth in a cauftic ftate, (or *quick-lime*) exhibits none of the above figns of an alkaline hepar fulphuris. It is detected how-ever, by the addition of alkali, which pre-cipitates the calcareous earth, and by form-ing a true hepar fulphuris, the waters then begin to affume the qualities enumerated in the preceding paragraph.

To difcover Foffile Oil in Waters.

THIS is generally found floating on their furface, but may be blended with the water by means of an alkali, or quick-lime, in form of a foap.

Such waters will curdle on the addition of acids, juft the fame as hard waters do with foap.

G

. To difcover Calcareous Earth in Waters.

THIS is foluble in water;

1. By being deprived of fixed air, or in the ftate of quick-lime, which is very well known from the manner of making lime water; from which the calcareous earth is again precipitated on reftoring fixed air, as, *e. g.* in breathing into the water through a tube.

There is a quantity of fixed air generated in refpiration *, and this mode of trial may fufficiently ferve; but befides this there is another method made ufe of—Fixed air produced from the effervefcence of an acid with an alkali, or with chalk, may be received into a bladder and afterwards made to pafs through the water to be examined in a gentle ftream: if the water contains a calcareous earth, it will be precipitated, by the fixed air rendering it unfoluble.

---

* Dr. *Priefly* fuppofes that the fixed air produced in refpiration is not thrown off from the lungs, but is precipitated from the common air by means of the phlogifton extricated in refpiration.

The *argillaceous, ochrey,* and *flinty* earths can only be fufpended or diffufed, and cannot therefore conftitute any impregnation in waters.

To difcover Selenites in Water.

SELENITES, or gypfum, *(vid. table of earthy falts,)* which is the matter of all hard waters, is difcovered,

1. By the well known effect of fuch waters in curdling foap.

2. By the evaporation of thefe waters thin laminous chryftals, like the fcales of fifhes, may be obtained, of a rough aftringent tafte, which are difficultly foluble.

3. By adding a folution of mercury in the nitrous acid a turbith mineral is formed, as before explained *(vid. page 7.)*

To difcover Epfom Salts, and Magnefia, in Waters.

EPSOM SALTS, compofed of the vitriolic acid and magnefia, *(vid. table,)* are obtained from waters by evaporation and chryftallization, in the fame manner as Glauber's falts, from which they are eafily diftinguifhed.

1. By the precipitation of magnefia on adding an alkali: Glauber's falts having no alkaline bafe fuffers no decompofition.

2. By their not being fufible as Glauber's falts.

They are diftinguifhed from common falt,

1. By giving out no fumes on the addition of oil of vitriol, *(vid. page 7.)*

To difcover Alum in Waters.

1. ALUM in waters fhew many of the figns of an acid, *(vid. page 16.)*

2. By evaporating waters that contain an alum, they acquire a rough auftere tafte.

3. An alkali added to au aluminous water, precipitates the earth in *floculi,* or little curdled clouds, (not in a powder) which, if too much alkali be not made ufe of, will be rediffolved by the fuperabundant quantity of the vitriolic acid which alum contains.

To difcover the Metallic Contents of Mineral Waters.

IRON:—The common tefts of the pre-fence of iron are powdered galls, or tincture of galls in brandy, and the phlogifticated al-kali *. Waters containing iron, with the tincture of galls, ftrike a purple or black co-lour: fometimes the addition of a minute portion of alkali is neceffary to make this experiment fucceed. The trial with the phlogifticated alkali is a much more accu-rate and pleafing one; the waters which contain iron ftrike with this a beautiful Pruffian blue.

Iron being diffolved in waters by feveral different means, the fame tefts do not uni-verfally apply.

I. Waters which contain iron, diffolved by fixed air, drop it on the efcape of the air;

---

* The *phlogifticated alkali*, or Pruffian alkali, as it is called, (becaufe of its ufe in the manufacture of Pruffian blue,) is made by the calcination of tartar and bullocks blood. The alkali of the tartar is thus charged with a quantity of inflammable matter, and is faid to be *phlogifticated.*——For the explanation of the procefs by which Pruffian blue is formed. *Vid. Macquer's Dictionnaire de Chemie.*

hence the difficulty of tranfporting many of the chalybeate waters.

II. Waters containing iron, diffolved by the volatile fulphureous acid, likewife quickly lofe their properties by ftanding, but at firft are to be tried as the following, *viz.*

III. Thofe that contain a vitriol or iron, diffolved by the common vitriolic acid.

Martial vitriol in waters is afcertained,

1. By tincture of galls and phlogifticated alkali.
: 2. By alkali or calcareous earth, which precipitate an ochre.
3. By evaporation; fome waters, as Hartfell, affording chryftals.

IV. Waters that contain iron, by means of an hepar fulphuris, are known,

1. By their fmell.
2. By their not depofiting any ochre on the addition of alkali.
3. By their not affording chryftals on e-vaporation.

V. Waters that contain iron by means of a calcareous hepar fulphuris;

1. Afford no chryftals on evaporation.

2. Drop an ochre with cauftic (though not with mild alkali) it will have no fmell.

To difcover Copper in Waters.

1. THE Pruffian alkali precipitates copper, from waters containing it, in a *red* powder.

2. Volatile alkali, added to waters containing copper, gives them a fine blue or fapphire colour.

3. An iron wire immerfed in a cupreous water is tranfmuted into copper; the vitriolic acid, which keeps the copper diffolved in the water, having a greater attraction for the iron, takes that up, and depofits the copper in its place *.

---

* It is faid that the waters of *Wisklow* in *Ireland* contain fo much copper, that they obtain in this way a quantity fufficient to become an article of fale.

To difcover Zinc in Waters.

ZINC is precipitated from waters by the Pruffian alkali, in the form of a *white* powder.

By proper evaporation chryftals of white vitriol may be obtained, for it is in the form of a vitriol, or diffolved by the vitriolic acid, that this femi-metal is found in waters.

SECTION II.

I. ON THE BATH WATERS.

THESE hot fprings, fituated in the eaft end of the ifland, were firft difcovered about the year 1695, and foon after being found to be a powerful remedy in the cure of the dry belly-ache and fome other prevailing difeafes of the climate, they were purchafed by the country, with the adjacent lands, for the public ufe; an hofpital was founded for the reception of poor people, and it was the objeＣt of the legiﬂature, in order to make the place of the utmoſt poﬄible benefit to the Iﬂand, to eſtabliſh a townſhip ; accordingly commiﬄioners were appointed, who were formed into a body corporate, veſted with authority for granting of lands and making the neceﬀary laws and regulations reſpeＣting the town and the bath. The public deſign was much promoted by the zeal and liberal donations of ſome private gentlemen, particularly of *Peter Valette*, Eſq. (whoſe public and benevolent charaＣter is too well known in this Iﬂand to require any Eulogium) and the place began to be viſited, not merely on account of the ſalubrity of the waters, but as a faſhionable ſejour.

Nothing could have obſtruＣted the progreſs of this town, or hindered the completion of the public plan, but the unfortunate political faＣtions that prevailed in the country during its infant ſtate ; which deſtroying the harmony of private life, prevented the principal families from reſorting here as formerly, and the place has ſince that time fallen into conſiderable decline. The Houſe of Aﬄem

G

bly has, neverthelefs, not fuffered the public to be deprived of the benefit of the waters by withholding any neceffary grants for the keeping up of roads and buildings to make the place be conveniently vifited by invalids; and the liberal fum they have lately given for thefe ufes, it is hoped, will, by rendering the baths more convenient, and the place more agreeable, caufe a greater conflux of company to it. There are befides many other circumftances that concur in inviting people to the place, and in removing the objections that were formerly made againft it; amongft which I fhall firft mention the advantage of a better road, in confequence of the late turnpike act; next to that of the change of of climate, which was formerly, in this neighbourhood, fo exceedingly rainy as to be hardly habitable: the quantity of rain which has been known to fall in a given time, (to perfons not acquainted with the Weft-Indies, and have not feen what are called the *feafons,*) would feem incredible,— above 40 perpendicular inches have fallen in about the fpace of 6 or 8 hours, which is nearly double the quantity that, on a medium, falls in Great-Britain through a whole year. The progrefs of cultivation having occafioned the falling of the adjacent woods, has produced a great alteration in the ftate of the feafons, particular years excepted, as the laft, which was a very wet one over al-moft the whole Ifland.

Laftly, I muft not omit to mention the Botanic Garden inftituted here about five years ago, which is already in a flourifhing ftate, being ftocked with a great variety of the moft rare and ufeful plants collected from every quarter of the globe, and cannot there-fore fail of furnifhing out a great deal of en-tertainment not only to the cultivators of na-tural fcience, but to every one vifiting the place.

Analyfis of the Bath Waters.

THE waters (for there are feveral fprings) iffue from fundry clefts and fiffures in the rocks on the fide of a fmall river, called from thence the *Sulphur River,* whofe fource is in that ftupendous pile of mountains which run eaft and weft through the Ifland : the feveral fprings are fituated very near to each other,

no others of the same nature having been discovered in the neighbourhood; in the parish
of Portland indeed, (on the oppofite fide of
the great ridge) there is a fmall one of the
fame kind, but of weaker impregnation, and
lower temperature.

There appears to be no difference in the
waters iffuing from the feveral fprings, except in their temperature, which is in fome
of them ten or twelve degrees lefs than in
the principal one, which forms a current of
nearly four inches diameter, and fupplies the
baths on the oppofite fide of the river.

The water when received into a glafs at
the fountain fide is perfectly tranfparent, but
has a fœtid fulphureous fmell and tafte.
which it retains in fome degree for feveral
hours; this however ultimately flies off without any change or precipitation; and the
water afterwards appears to be a very pure
common water *.

---

* This water is extremely well fitted for bottling, and proves
not inferior to Briftol water: The late Dr. M'Kenzie, who refided
for fome time at this place, had fome of it by him in bottles for
feveral years, which remained perfectly fweet and good.

The immediate effects which follow on drinking the bath waters are, frequent eructations of wind, fometimes a degree of Vertigo or head-ache, and ficknefs at the ftomach ; a copious flow of perfpiration and urine ; after which an exhilaration of mind generally enfues, with an encreafe of appetite, and at night natural reft.

G R A V I T Y.

THE fpecific gravity of the water appears to vary a good deal from that of common water, as will be feen from the following experiments ; when taken from the fpring it is indeed lighter, on account of its heat and other caufes, than common water, but cooled to the fame point it becomes heavier, from the earthy and faline matter with which it is impregnated.

E X P E R I M E N T S.

1. AN *hydrometrical* gauge plunged into the Bath waters, taken as hot as poffible from the fpring, funk 4 inches 5-10ths.

2. The above mentioned inftrument funk in common water heated to the fame 'point, *(viz.* about 125 deg.) only 3 inches 6-10ths.

3. The fame gauge funk in the Bath water, when cold, 1 inch 3-10ths.

4. The fame gauge funk in the river water 1 inch 5-10ths.

The Bath water is therefore to common water, when hot, as 45 to 36, when cold, as 13 to 15.

By weighing it as accurately as I could with a common beam, I found the gravity of the Bath water to exceed that of the river 1 drahm and 20 grains in the pint.

It feems extraordinary that the Bath waters fhould, when hot, be lighter than common water of the fame temperature, and when cold, heavier; I can only explain it from the phlogifton which it contains, many waters become heavier after a decompofition takes place in their component principles: The Buxton waters, *e. gr.* placed in an exhaufted receiver, gave out no air bubbles,

but turned whitifh, and weighed 16 grains
in the pint heavier immediately after, *(vid.
Monro on Mineral Waters).*

TEMPERATURE.

THE temperature of the feveral fprings, fo
far as my obfervations have reached, is uni-
formly the fame under all the differences of
weather and variations of the atmofphere;
though, if we may credit the experiments
made by gentlemen fome years ago, the water appears to have been hotter than I have
ever found it, and to have varied a few degrees in its temperature, at different times.

FAHRENHEIT.

Heat of the main fpring by my ther-
mometer,   -   -   127
Ditto of the low fpring,   ..   -   124
Ditto of the upper do.   -   -   114
Ditto of the higheft do.   -   -   112
Ditto of the water running from the
guttering into the baths,   -   -   122
Ditto of the water brought in a four
gallon jug to the town, diftant
nearly two miles,   -   -   118

It might be expected, that I fhould here explain the caufes of heat in thefe fprings, but the common hypothefis concerning the generation of hot waters is very unfatisfactory, and I fhall not prefume to offer any of my own : It may be fufficient to obferve, that the heat of fome waters is entirely adventitious, not owing to any principles which they contain, but acquired by pafling through ftrata in the vicinity of volcanos or heated matters. Others appear to owe their heat either to fome union or decompofition in the foffile matters through which the waters pafs, and by which they become impregnated ; the nature of this union or decompofition may be various, but has never been clearly underftood, unlefs perhaps in the cafe of pyrites, on which the heat of the thermæ, or hot fprings, is fuppofed moft commonly to depend.

Experiments to afcertain the Contents of the
Bath Waters.

EXPERIMENT I.

THE Bath water, placed in the exhauſt-
ed receiver of the air pump, gave out
very few air bubbles.

Having no air-pump I could not make
this experiment myſelf; but it was tried
ſome years ago by a medical gentleman *,
who anylyſed the Moffat Waters in this
neighbourhood, and I believe with ſufficient
accuracy.

EXPERIMENT II. A bottle filled with
the Bath water immediately from the fountain, had an oiled bladder tied over the
mouth of it, after which it was placed in a
veſſel of hot water : The heat of the water
being encreaſed to the boiling point, a ſmall
quantity of air was ſeparated, which was ſe-
cured by tying a ligature round the neck of
the bladder, and afterwards made to paſs in

. * The account of this analyſis is *anorymous*, but I am informed it was wrote by Dr. *Mitchell*, formerly a practitioner in *Blue*
Mountain Valley.

H

a gentle ftream through lime-water; but no precipitation enfued, as happened by breathing through the fame lime-water (*vid.* p. 30.)

The Bath waters have been fuppofed to contain a confiderable quantity of fixed air*, but from what circumftance I cannot conceive, as they are totally deftitute of that fparkling appearance and poignant tafte that diftinguifh fuch waters, and the above experiments plainly demonftrate that they have no fuch impregnation.

EXPERIMENT III. A bottle accurately filled with the Bath water was inverted in a veffel full of the fame water, fo as to allow no air to enter the bottle; the veffel with the water in this pofition was then placed over the fire, and the heat of the water encreafed to the boiling point,—the water in the bottle was obferved to defcend about half an inch; but on fuffering it to cool, it afcended again, fo as to leave no vacuum in the bottle.

---

* *Vid.* Hiftory of Jamaica.

EXPERIMENT IV. A bottle filled with the water was clofely ftopped by a cork, which was perforated by a crooked tube, the other end of which entered an inverted phial filled with water, and placed in a veffel of water after the manner of Dr. *Prieftly*: Being allowed thus to remain for 24 hours, there was no defcent of the water in the phial.

The two laft experiments ferve to fhew that the Bath waters contain no air of any kind, unlefs a fmall quantity of common or atmofpheric air, which I apprehend was what was extricated in experiment II. and III.—It is hence doubtful if the Bath waters contain any phlogifticated or inflammable air as has been fuppofed.

EXPERIMENT V. Some of the fine blue flowers of a convolvulus were infufed for an hour or two in the Bath water without fuffering any change in their colour; on adding a fingle drop of the oil of vitriol, the colour of the flowers was immediately changed from a blue to a bright red.

EXPERIMENT VI. Some drops of oil of tartar being added to a glafs of the Bath water, no effervefcence or other change enfued.

EXPERIMENT VII. Some drops of a folution of hepar fulphuris being added to a glafs of the Bath water, no lactefcence was produced, till I dropped in a little oil of vitriol.

EXPERIMENT VIII. Some drops of an unfaturated folution of lead in the nitrous acid, were added to a glafs of Bath water *, which effected no alteration.

EXPERIMENT IX. Some drops of a folution of mercury in the nitrous acid were added to a glafs of the Bath water, no yellow precipitation enfued †.

From thefe experiments (N° 5, 6, 7, 8, 9,) it is very apparent that the Bath waters contain no vitriolic acid (*vid.* page 31) in a feparate ftate.

---

* See this experiment explained, page 34.
† Ditto   do.   do.   page 37.

EXPERIMENT X. Some drops of the oil of vitriol were added to a glafs of the Bath water, no ebullition or effervefcence enfued.

In the account given of the Bath waters in the hiftory of Jamaica, it is faid, that a-cids dropped into the Bath water caufe an ebullition ; but it is certainly a miftake, and I believe it has arifen from the obferver not rightly diftinguifhing between an ebullition and the difficult mixture of the acid and the water; the acid, being fo very ponderous, on being dropped into the water falls through it, and caufes an appearance that might be miftaken for an effervefcence, by perfons not properly acquainted with the fubject.

EXPERIMENT XI. A folution of fal mar-tis being dropped into the Bath water, no ochrous precipitation followed, (*vid.* p. 35, fec. 4.)

EXPERIMENT XII. Some drops of a nice-ly faturated folution of chalk in the nitrous acid were added to a glafs of Bath water, but no precipitation enfued, (*vid.* p. 35, fec. 3.)

Thefe experiments, (N° 10, 11, 12,) clearly fhew that there is no alkali in the Bath water, (*vid.* p. 35.) but left the alkali might be in too diffufed a ftate to be difcovered by the above tefts, I repeated the experiments on the water after confiderable evaporation, and the refult was the fame.

EXPERIMENT XIII. To the Bath waters I added a fmall portion of alkaline falt, and obferved no change, but the fame experiment being tried, after evaporating the water a little, a white precipitation followed, (*vid.* p. 14.)

EXPERIMENT XIV. A few drops of a faturated folution of lead in the nitrous acid, added to the Bath water, caufed a milkinefs, (*vid.* p. 14.)

The fame effect followed on adding a clear folution of faccharum faturni.

EXPERIMENT 15. The water during evaporation, with a very gentle heat, depofited a quantity of reddifh brown earth, which I feparated by decanting the liquor from time to time as it collected at the bottom of the veffel.

EXPERIMENT XVI. To the earthy pre-cipitate obtained in the preceding experi-ment, I added fome diftilled water, but on-ly a part of it diffolved.

EXPERIMENT XVII. To the foregoing precipitate repeatedly wafhed in frefh quan-tities of diftilled water, I added fome drops of the oil of vitriol, which caufed a flight effervefcence ; but great part of it remained undiffolved, which was alfo infoluble in the nitrous acid, and with difficulty foluble in water.

EXPERIMENT XVIII. After further eva-poration of the water I placed it at reft for 12 hours, and then found it covered with thin laminous chryftals like the fcales of fifhes, which being taken off and put in dif-tilled water, great part of them continued to float therein, remaining undiffolved for fome days : the tafte of thefe chryftals was rough and earthy, not faline. Thefe are the proper-ties of the felenitic compound (vid. p. 8); which the following experiment more clear-ly demonftrate them to have been.

EXPERIMENT XIX. To a folution of the chryftals (exp. 18) in diftilled water, I added fome drops of the folution of mercury in the nitrous acid, which caufed a yellow precipi-- tation (*vid.* p. 37, fec. 5.)

EXPERIMENT XX. That portion of the earth which was diffolved by the vitriolic acid in experiment 15, was precipitated again by adding a few drops of oil of tartar. I wafhed the precipitate in diftilled water, and then re-diffolved it in frefh vitriolic acid; the liquor formed thereby was bitter and fa- line, refembling that of epfom falts.

I repeated this folution and precipitation feveral times, fo as to leave no doubt of the earth being a *magnefia.*

The foregoing experiments made on the earth precipitated during evaporation, were all repeated on the refiduum left after evapo- ration to drynefs, with nearly the fame re- fult, only that I found it difficult to obtain the earth entirely pure, fome of the faline matter adhering, notwithftanding repeated affufions of diftilled water.

Magnefia in waters is generally combined
with the vitriolic acid, conftituting epfom
falts ; but as there are no figns of vitriolic
acid in this water, unlefs in the felenitic
compound, it is not improbable that the
magnefia is blended with the fea falt, which
this water appears, from the fubfequent experiments, to contain, forming with the muriatic acid a fixed ammoniac (*vid.* p. 8. fec. 3.)

EXPERIMENT XXI. On dropping a folution of filver in the nitrous acid into the
Bath water, a white curdled precipitation
immediately took place, (*vid.* p. 38. fec. 4.)

EXPERIMENT XXII. The precipitate in
the preceding experiment, with a little tartar, being rubbed on polifhed brafs, gave it,
by the affiftance of heat, a filver colour *.

Having thefe evident proofs, (experiment
20, 19,) of the prefence of muriatic falt, I en-
deavoured to obtain it in its chryftallized ftate.

EXPERIMENT XXIII. A quantity of the
refiduum was diffolved in diftilled water,

---

* This precipitate called a *Luna Cornea* is the fubftance made
ufe of by artifts for fome kinds of filvering.

I

and the liquor decanted clear from the earthy fediment, which was then flowly evaporated, firft by the fire, and then by the fun. Regular cubical chryftals were thus obtained, having all the properties of common falt, (*vid.* p. 37.)

EXPERIMENT XXIII. A portion of the refiduum (experiment 15,) being thrown on a hot iron, gave out no fumes or fmell of fulphur.

EXPERIMENT XXIV. The incruftation adhering to the rocks about the fpring was alfo burnt, but yielded no proofs of its containing any fulphur.

EXPERIMENT XXV. A new coined bright dollar was placed in the water at the place of its iffue, which in a few minutes was tarnifhed of a deep purple colour,—a bright piece of gold coin was turned of a deep copper colour. The fame trials being made at the extremity of the gutturing, where the water is difcharged into the Baths, the metals were but flightly tarnifhed after lying a confiderable time,

EXPERIMENT XXVI. Having made certain characters on paper with the sympathetic ink, (*i. e.* a solution of saccharum saturni in water) I tied the paper over a broad mouthed bottle filled with the Bath water, the vapours of which soon rendered the characters visible.

EXPERIMENT XXVII. Saccharum saturni dissolved in the Bath water causes no red or brown precipitation.

Thefe experiments (N° 23 and 24) prove that the Bath waters contain no actual sulphur (*vid.* p. 39); but the following ones (N° 25 and 26) evidently shew the presence of the phlogiston in some form (*vid.* p. 40): Why experiment 27 does not succeed I cannot tell, unless from the phlogistic principle being so very volatile as not to remain long enough to produce the effect.

The fætor of these waters indicate the presence of a hepar sulphuris (*vid.* p. 40); but this is rendered doubtful by the experiments made with acids (*vid.* experiment 10) which cause no precipitation, and others shewing that the waters contain no alkali.

From what has been faid (*vid.* p. 41) concerning hepar fulphuris with quick-lime, it
is obvious that fulphur cannot be fufpected
in the Bath waters, in this form.

In what ftate of combination then, are we
to fuppofe the phlogifton exiftent in thefe
waters? According to the late difcoveries, refpecting the various fpecies of phlogifticated
air, it feemed exceedingly probable that it
was in fome fuch form : This opinion feems,
however, overturned by experiment 2d and
3d, in which I found it impoffible to obtain any air that was permanent.

The mode of combination muft ftill remain a defideratum, as chemiftry has not,
that I know of, found out any other methods
of trial for afcertaining it.

Before I difmifs this fubject I muft not
omit taking notice of Dr. *Brown's* hypothefis concerning thefe waters, (*vid. the Natural
Hiftory of Jamaica)* which is, that they contain the volatile vitriolic acid connected with
a calcareous earth : they certainly contain

jelenites, but this affords no explanation refpecting the phlogiston. Befides, how the
volatile acid can be fuppofed combined with
the calcareous earth, I do not conceive; for
felenites is one of the moft fixed falts we
know of. As he has taken no notice of any
of the other contents of thefe waters, which
were very obvious on the flighteft trial, I
fufpect that he never made any experiment
on them, but fpoke merely from conjecture.

EXPERIMENT XXVIII. Into a glafs of
the Bath water I dropped a fmall quantity of
the tincture of galls in brandy; no apparent
change took place after ftanding fome time,
till I added a folution of iron, when it immediately affumed a deep purple colour. ·

EXPERIMENT XXIX. I repeated the foregoing experiment, ufing, inftead of the galls,
the phlogifticated alkali; but no effect followed till I added the iron, when the ufual
beautiful blue precipitation immediately took
place (*vid.* p. 45.)

It is hence (*viz.* from N° 28 and 29) obvious, that thefe waters have no metallic

impregnation, though they have been generally fuppofed to contain fome iron; and
Mr. L—— (*vid. Hift. Jamaica*) fays, that
there is an ochrey precipitation about the
rocks over which the waters run. The yellow
flimy incruftation about the rocks may have
fomething of the appearance of an ochre, but
from the following experiment it does not
feem to contain any iron.

Experiment XXX. I took a quantity
of the above mentioned flimy matter, adhering about the rocks where the fpring is,
which having firft dried in the fun, I mixed
with oil and charcoal duft, and placed it in
the ftrong heat of a furnace for fome hours;
a blackifh gritty powder was found in the
crucible, which was not in the leaft affected by the magnet.

Experiment XXXI. I then fubjected it
to the fire without any admixture, fufpect-
ing that it was of a vegetable origin, and
would yield a pot-afh; after keeping it for
a confiderable time in a very violent heat, I
obtained a powder refembling brick duft,

reddiſh and gritty; a part of this powder effervefced with acids and diffolved, but moſt of it retained its gritty form. Pot-aſh being at firſt in a cauſtic ſtate, this experiment muſt not be tried immediately after removing it from the furnace, unlefs you throw in fixed air to the water you mix it with.

I infer from the foregoing experiment, (N° 31) that the flimy matter of the rock is partly of a vegetable nature, produced by the putrefaction of leaves, &c. falling into the water, and partly ſtoney, fome particles of fand and rock being entangled in it.

EXPERIMENT XXXII. *On the Rock.—* The rock being kept for fome time in a ſtrong heat, was partly converted into quick-lime.

EXPERIMENT XXXIII. The rock powdered and mixed with charcoal, &c. as in experiment 30,—ſhewed no figns of iron; fome of the iron ore in the neighbourhood being tried in the fame manner, was afterwards attracted very ſtrongly by the magnet.

Having thus related and explained my feveral experiments made on the Bath waters,
I fhall next, after fumming up the refults
in a general table, proceed to fhew their effects on the human body, and their cure in
difeafes.

Table of Experiments and Refults.

EXPERIMENTS.		RESULTS.
N°. 1, 2, 3, -		*No fixed air.*
— 1, 2, 3, 4, -		*No inflammable air.*
— 5, 6, 7, 8, 9,		*No feparate acid.*
— 10, 11, 12, -	Seer that the BATH WATERS contain	*No feparate alkali.*
— 13, 14, 15, 16,		
17, 18, -		*A felenetic falt.*
— 20, - - -		*Earth of magnefia.*
— 21, 22, - -		*Common marine falt.*
— 23, 24, - -		*No actual fulphur.*
— 25, 26, - -		*A good deal of phlogifton*
— 10, 11, 12, -		*No hepar fulphuris.*

CHAPTER IV.

On the Effects and Uses of the Bath Waters.

HAVING learned by analyfis the matters contained in mineral waters, we
can fometimes with certainty determine, *a
priori,* what will be their effect on the human body; but not univerfally; for notwithftanding the feveral principles of a water may
be clearly detected, yet their mode of combination being unknown, their ufes can only
be conjectured, till experience has afcertained
them. The Somerfetfhire Bath Waters, *e. g.*
contain, according to the lateft and beft analyfis by Dr. *Faulkener* and others, *a little
common falt, fome hepar fulphuris with
quick-lime, a minute portion of iron,* (viz.
*only one 37th of a grain in a pint of the
water) fome felenites and fixed air.* However
active thefe principles may be, I apprehend
it will be impoffible, from the fmall pro-
portion they contain of each, to account fully
for their extenfive influence in the cure of
difeafes. There will be as much difficulty
in accounting fatisfactorily for the operation

K

of our waters; yet from comparing their effects together, their general action feems to
be *ftimulant*; which power they owe chiefly to
the fulphureous gas, or phlogiftic principle,
the fixed contents being in too fmall a quantity to be productive of any material operation.

That the Bath waters act as a ftimulant is
very obvious from the immediate effects
which the drinking of them produce, *viz.*
eructations of wind, vertigo, head-ache, and
fever, &c. &c. *(viz.* p. 53) as well as from
the nature of feveral difeafes in which they
are found remedial.

Dr. *Brown*, in his Natural Hiftory of the
Ifland, fays of thefe waters, " that they are
" remarkably beneficial in all capillary ob-
" ftructions or diforders proceeding from
" weaknefs or the want of proper glandular
" fecretions ; in all lentors or vifcidities pro-
" ceeding from the inaction of the folid fyf-
" tem ; in confumptions, nervous fpafms
" and weakneffes : They reftore the appetite
" and ufual action of the vifcera, invigorate

" the circulation, warm the juices, open the
" fkin and urinary paffages, ftrengthen the
" nerves, and feldom fail of producing eafy
" fleep at night.

Mr. L * * * *, in his well wrote Hiftory of the Ifland, gives nearly the fame account of thefe waters ;—He fays, " they
" excite appetite, promote urine, produce
" fleep, cure ulcers, ftrengthen the nerves,
" and cure palfey.

Thefe effects, moft of which I have feen
verified in a great number of cafes, evidently
indicate a ftimulant power. 1ftly, The expulfion of flatulencies, increafe of appetite,
&c. fhew that the water excites the action of
the ftomach. 2dly, The vertigo, head-ache,
and fever, which they fometimes induce, are
confequent on an encreafed circulation. 3dly,
Their diuretic effects, in like manner, proceed from their ftimulant action on the kidneys : their operation in this refpect, is in
part owing to the quantity taken in as a diluent, but they have certainly a further effect than as a mere diluent; for in fome,

çafes * the quantity of urine difcharged has greatly exceeded the whole quantity of fluid made ufe of. 4thly, An increafe of perfpiration may be varioufly accounted for; 1ftly, the waters may prove diaphoretic from their action in the ftomach, between which and the extreme veffels of the body there is a particular confent: 2dly, They muft be diaphoretic as being diluent; but befides, they may, 3dly, from their fulphureous contents, act as a ftimulant in the extreme capillary veffels.

Whether the Bath waters may not alfo have fome *alterant* and *antifpafmodic* power, I fhall not determine, but it would feem probable that they are poffeffed of both.

 Having faid thus much to explain the general nature and action of the Bath Waters, I fhall now confider their ufes in particular difeafes.

I. The *Dry Belly-ache* feems to have been the complaint in which the good effects of the Bath waters were firft moft eminently ex-

---

* I am obliged to my friend Dr. *Clarke* for a very particular cafe of this nature.

perienced, and they have ever fince been applied to as a moft fovereign remedy againft
the paralytic torpor and relaxation that fu-
pervene to the excruciating fpafms which by
turns affect the bowels and limbs of people
in this horrid difeafe. I muft not in this
place enter largely into the confideration of
either the caufes or cure of this complaint;
but whatever it depends on, whether on the
action of any poifon taken in (as of lead, a-
cid, ardent fpirit, &c.) on an acrimonious
bile in the firft paffages, or on a conftriction
of the furface from cold, concurring with an
irritable ftate of the bowels, it is obvious,
that, after removing the conftipation, the
principal indication of cure is to reftore the
loft tone. As *fpafm*, or a violent ftate of
contraction in the mufcular fibres, produces
the alternate ftate of *atonia* or relaxation, fo
vice verfa, atonia gives occafion to the return of fpafm : Accordingly we fee that patients, once affected with this diforder, are
fubject to frequent relapfes, which nothing
can fo effectually prevent, as exciting the action of the inteftinal canal. With this view
various medicines are employed, but the

Bath waters have been found, of all others, the moſt uſeful remedy : Their effects in ſuch caſes ſeem almoſt miraculous.

The uſe of the Hot Baths jointly with the waters, 1ſt, by the grateful ſtimulus they impart to the nervous ſyſtem, and, 2d, by cauſing a free determination to the ſurface, contribute greatly in removing the torpor and palſey of the extremities.

II. *Genuine Palſey*, or *Hæmiplegia*, is a a diſorder totally of a different nature from the preceding. There is in this caſe an affection of the brain, or of the nerves in their origin; but notwithſtanding ſuch a diſſimilitude, the Bath waters may, in conjunction with other remedies, prove extremely beneficial. A remarkable inſtance has lately occurred of the efficacy of the Bath waters in paralytic diſorders,—A gentleman under recovery from a long fever, by expoſure to cold air, ſuddenly loſt the uſe of all his limbs ; Having tried the uſe of ſeveral remedies with little effect, he had recourſe to the Bath waters, by which he was in a few weeks perfectly recovered.

III. The ufe of the Bath waters is highly conducive to *convalefcents* of every clafs, efpecially after fevers : By exciting appetite and invigorating the bowels, it reftores the tone of the whole fyftem, and obviates a tendency to relapfe.

IV. The effects which the Bath waters have on the nervous fyftem, and in affifting the functions of the ftomach, fhew them to be a very fit remedy in all *hyfterical* and *fexual* complaints.

V. I fhall next confider how far the Bath waters are ufeful in *vifceral obftructions*, or in complaints of the liver and fpleen ; patients labouring under thefe complaints have frequently had recourfe to thefe waters, and, I believe, have not always been difappointed of receiving benefit, but I neverthelefs think that in fuch complaints they are rather an ambiguous remedy : So far as they ftrengthen the functions of the ftomach and the bowels they may be ufeful, but from their ftimulant or heating quality, they may femetimes do hurt by exciting inflammation. Perfons who have undergone a mercurial regimen for the removal of thefe complaints, may, however, derive great advantage from the waters: The danger of topical inflammation being removed, the ufe of them will afterwards contribute much to their recovery. This leads me to fpeak of their effects after falivation in other diforders.

VI. Mercury, though the only certain remedy which fome difeafes admit of, is neverthelefs an hazardous one; under the moft careful management it fometimes makes great depredations in the conftitution, particularly in warm climates, where the tone of the fyftem being once impaired, is difficultly recovered. In this view, and for removing fome fymptoms, which mercury of itfelf is not a cure for, the Bath waters are highly beneficial in the lues venerea: They ferve to fupport the general health, and perhaps affift in wafhing out the venereal virus. With the Hot Baths they are of great ufe in relieving the nocturnal pains, cleaning and curing the ulcers, eruptions, &c. &c.

They have in fome inftances difcovered a
fingular efficacy in ftopping old *gleets* *.
They may operate in two ways in the cure of
fuch complaints; 1ft, as a diluent in wafhing
out fome latent virus; or, 2dly, by their tonic
power in the ftomach, and in bracing up the
whole fyftem. It is, however, immaterial
how they act, if they produce the effect,
which is unqueftionable : I have no doubt of
their proving equally fo in the *fluor albus*.

VII. The Bath waters are not only ferviceable in the lues venerea, but alfo in that
more loathfome diftemper of negroes, the
yaws : By the drinking of the waters, and
the ufe of the hot baths, the eruption is
thrown out more plentifully on the furface of the body, and the matter eliminated;
by which the internal fyftem feems to be relieved, and the cure expedited. Nothing
can be more pernicious than the general
practice of negroes in this diforder, I mean

---

* Dr. *Irvine*, a gentleman univerfally known for his many virtues, as well as by his long refidence in this neighbourhood, has
favoured me with a very fingular cafe of this kind, where a per-
fon was cured by the Bath waters of a gleet of eleven years ftanding.—I know of fome other cafes almoft as fingular,

that of wafhing in the cold rivers. The furface being by that means conftringed, the
yaws are repelled, which I believe is frequently the caufe of fubfequent bone-ache and
diftortion.

VIII. Every kind of cutaneous diftemper
may receive advantage from the Bath waters.
An inveterate *leprofy* was relieved by it; but
I apprehend that in cutaneous defœdations
there may be found waters ftill more ufeful
than thofe of the Bath. Their ufe in abflerging
and drying up foul ulcers, is fo well known
I fhall fay nothing on the fubject.

IX. Dr. *Brown* mentions *confumption* a-
mong the difeafes in which the Bath waters
are ufeful; but if he means a confumption
of the lungs, I fhould fear he is miftaken:
Confidering the degree of phlogiftic diathefis,
or inflammatory difpofition that prevails in
this difeafe, I conceive the Bath waters may
rather tend to aggravate than relieve the
fymptoms; but I have no experience, and
have not been able to collect any facts on the
fubject.

X. I fhould not either fuppofe the Bath waters indicated in *dropfy*, but a cure in that diforder has been obtained by fuch various and even oppofite means, that I fhould not think the trial of them improper where o-ther remedies have failed. The Bath waters being poffeffed of an active principle, capable of producing material changes in the fyf-tem, may accidentally excite the action of the abforbent veffels, and caufe the waters to be carried off by the different outlets of the body:

XI. In the *jaundice* they are ufeful after the obftruction in the biliary ducts is removed, for carrying off the bile in the circulation, and for ftrengthening the impaired functions of digeftion, &c.

XII. The diuretic effect of the Bath waters make them ufeful in *nephritic* complaints, in which they operate both as a diluent and by a fpecific quality without much ftimulus. In fuch *nephritic* affections as depend on a gouty diathefis, the Bath waters are calculated to anfwer extremely well;

which will be obvious from what I have to remark on their effects in the gout.

XIII. The gout is a difeafe depending not on a *morbid matter*, as has been commonly fuppofed by phyficians as well as others, but on a certain ftate of the moving fibres, which belongs to a particular temperament or conftitution that is frequently hereditary, being tranfmitted from father to fon in the fame way as a likenefs of features and other conftitutional peculiarities : Hence there is no cure to be obtained in the gout but by obviating the effects of this particular temperament, which is only done in one way, *viz.* by exercife and abftinence from animal food. The difeafe, as an *articular affection*, feems falutary, tending to preferve the conftitution ; but when it becomes irregular and mifplaced, it is then dangerous and deftructive. Every cafe of irregular and mifplaced gout probably depends on the want of a neceffary degree of tone in the ftomach, to determine the affection to the extremities. We from hence fee how the Bath waters are ferviceable in the gout. The waters and hot baths, by exciting the action of the stomach, and of the extreme vessels, call back the gout to the joints, after being repelled, or determine it there, when wandering about the body.

When the constitution is much debilitated, and the gout occasions affections of the head and stomach particularly, instead of producing inflammation in the joints, it is called *atonic*; that is, from the want of *tone* the disease which should be seated in the extremities seizes on other parts, or is not able to form in the joints. In cases of this nature the Bath waters are very beneficial.

The inhabitants of the West-Indies make frequent voyages to Great-Britain on account of health when perhaps they have a remedy nearer at hand. In the atonic gout Dr. *Cullen* recommends a warm climate, and I therefore embrace the opportunity of suggesting to Jamaica gentlemen residing in Great-Britain, that under this disease they have in their own Island a climate more propitious, and in the Bath waters a remedy not less efficacious, and which deferved to be no lefs celebrated than thofe of England.

I might go on to illuftrate the effects of the Bath waters in a variety of other difeafes, but I fhall take notice of only one more, *viz.*

XV. *Chronical rheumatifm*, which figni-fies, habitual pains affecting particularly the large joints of the body without much fever, and fometimes with little fwelling, but with debility and coldnefs of the affected part. Rheumatic affections are the complaints of people in cold climates; but the inhabitants of the Weft-Indies are not exempt from them. Expofition to rain, night dews, and the north winds that blow at a particular feafon of the year, occafion fuch diforders, that are apt, notwithftanding every care and atten-tion to medicine, to return and become chro-nical. The Bath waters ftand very much recommended in fuch cafes, though at firft they feem to aggravate the difeafe, the pains being for fome time exafperated: By perfe-verance, however, the patient is fure of ob-taining relief.

Having, as I prefume, faid enough to fhew
the general utility of thefe Bath waters, and
to direct to the ufe and application of them;
nothing remains but to make a few remarks
on the method of ufing them.

Rules for the drinking of mineral waters
can only be general; they are neverthelefs of
ufe. The following ones are fuch as I think
more particularly require attention.

I. To begin the ufe of the waters with
fmall draughts, which may be repeated at
fhort intervals, as the fudden ingurgitation
of a large quantity may fometimes caufe un-
eafinefs and bad effects, (vid. p. 53.)

II. To ufe now and then a gentle laxative
as occafion may require, to prevent a confti-
pated ftate of the bowels.

III. To drink them as nearly to the fountain or place where they iffue, on account of
the extreme volatility of their medicinal principle, which is fo remarkable that it is com-
paratively of little ufe to drink them at any

diſtance ; they loſe even in their tranſporta-
tion acroſs the river *, *(vid.* p. 66, ſec. 4.)

IV. To continue the uſe of them for a due
length of time.

The character of any medicine being eſta-
bliſhed, people are commonly diſpoſed to
expect too much from it. There are inſtan-
ces where the effects of the Bath waters have
been manifeſted very ſuddenly, but in ſome
chronical caſes it is requiſite they ſhould be
perſiſted in for ſome length of time : Patients, after having deſpaired of obtaining
any relief, have, by perſeverance, obtained
a perfect recovery from the moſt inveterate
diſeaſes.

V. To uſe the hot baths in the afternoon
rather than in the morning, as they tend to
procure eaſe and ſleep : Care ſhould be ne-
vertheleſs taken to avoid cold on returning
from the Baths, and they ought not to be
uſed too ſoon after meals.

---

* The inconvenience which at preſent attends getting to the
ſpring will be ſoon removed by a bridge that is to be built acroſs
the river.

VI. Laftly, as to regimen.—I know of no
particular one required by the Bath waters.
It has been cuftomary to avoid wine and
fruits, not as I apprehend, from any difa-
greement thefe have with the waters, but becaufe they have not been fuited to the complaints for which the waters were drunk : A
little wine may be fometimes very neceffary,
but in general it is better totally to relin-
quifh it, as the precife limits are difficult to
be afcertained, and as it may interfere with
the ufe of the waters.

That I may omit nothing that can be of
ufe in directing to the application of thefe
waters, I fhall here fubjoin a catalogue of all
fuch difeafes as they are likely to prove beneficial in.

" *Quot et quam diverfi morbi curentur,*
" *thermarum et aquarum medicatarum ufu !*
" *Ad has confugere toties coquntur ægri, de-*
" *cantiffima alia remedia exterti abfque ullo*
" *fructu,* &c. *In* Thermis, *aqua nativo ca-*
" *lore laxat omnia & emollit, venis bibulis*
" *cutaneis fe infinuat, fanguini permifcetur,*

M

" *obftructa loca alluit ; et fi potentur fimul,*
" *falubres illæ aquæ, tutum et potens habetur*
" *remedium,* &c. &c." Vid. V. Swieten
Comm. Tom. III. page 345.

CATALOGUE of DISEASES,

in which the Bath Waters *are ufeful.*

ABORTION,
   (viz. after)
Anorexia, or want of
  appetite.
Afthma,
  1. *Nervous,* 2. *Gouty.*
Cancer.
Chorea, Sp. Vit. and
Cholera morbus,
  (viz. after)
Convulfions in general
Colic, *viz.*
  1. *Belly-ache,* 2. *Hy-*
  fterical, 3. *Gouty.*
Confumption, *(doubt-*
  ful.)

Crapula, or after fur-
  feits.
Deafnefs.
Dyfury, or pain and
  difficulty in paffing
  urine.
Elephantiafis.
Epilepfy.
Fevers, *(viz.* when
  recovering from, and
  to obviate a return
  of, particularly, ner-
  vous fevers.)
Flatulencies.
Fluor albus.
Gleets.

Green ficknels.

Gutta ferena.

Gout, *viz.* the atonic and irregular.

Herpes, impetigo, *&c.*

Hypochondria, and Hyfterics.

Jaundice.

Ifchias, or hip-gout

Ifchury, ftoppage of urine.

Lethargy. Leprofy.

Lues venerea, *vid.* p.

Lumbago, or rheuma-tifm in the loins.

Menfes (ad movendas)

Nephritis,

   1. *From Stone,*

   2. *From Gout.*

Palpitations.

Palfey, *vid.* p.

Poifons, (for recovery after)

Rheumatifm, *vid,* p.

Ricketts.

Salivation, (after)

Sterility.

Stone in the kidneys or bladder.

Strangury.

Stupor.

Suppreffion of urine.

Tendons contracted.

Tetanus, locked jaw.

Torpor.

Vertigo.

Ulcers, mali moris.

CATALOGUE of PATIENTS

who were either cured or greatly relieved by the drinking of the Bath Waters.

[Taken from a Memorandum-Book of *P. Valette*, Efq. kept by him for that purpofe before any Surgeon or Phyfician was appointed to the faid Bath.]

MR. B. Harris, cured of ————
Mr. G. Galbraith, of rheumatic pains.
Mr. M'Queen, of a lingering fever.
Mr. Rofs, of ditto.
Mr. James Watfon, of a dry belly-ache.—
  N. B. He was eafed by the firft draught of the water.
Mr. Alexander Grant, of the gravel.
John Gale, Efquire, of a lingering fever and lofs of appetite.
* William Hicks, Efq. of a fwelling in the fpleen.
John Gofling, of an intermittent.
John Robertfon, of ditto.
Charles Anfell, of a dry belly-ache.
Charles Webb, of a lingering fever.
Charles M'Farquhar, of a dry belly-ache.
Mr. Renny, of a lingering fever.
Mifs Barry, of a belly-ache with palfey of the limbs.
Mifs Gardiner, of a dry belly-ache and great weaknefs in the limbs.

Mrs. Puley, of a lingering fever and pain in the ftomach.

Mr. Jofeph Morris, of a dry belly-ache.

Mrs. Kilby, of lofs of appetite.

T. B. Ruffell, of a dry belly-ache.

Mr. Clarke, of the gravel.

John Pufey, Efq. of a lingering fever.

Mr. T. Fox, of the dry belly-ache and gravel.

Thomas Allan, of the dry belly-ache and confumption.

* Mr. Cargil, of the fciatica in four weeks.

Peter Carr, of ditto.

Mrs. Nelfon, of ditto.

Mrs. Forbes, of the hyfterics, and lofs of appetite and fleep.

* Capt. Jof. Lawrence, in one week greatly relieved of a fwelling of the fpleen and venereal ftrangury.

Mr. Maitland, of the rheumatifm.

Capt. J. Lawrence, of the gleet, ftrangury, &c.

Mrs. Garrioch, of a fwelling of the fpleen— Twice diffipated, and intermittent fever.

Mrs. M'Farquhar, of a belly-ache and weaknefs of the limbs.

* Mr. Alex. M'Farlane, of the fciatica.

Colonel Price, of a lingering fever, lofs of appetite and fleep,

Mr. S. Woolery, of a complication of diftempers.

Mr. Lawrence Brodbelt, of the gravel, when given over by the faculty and his friends.

Mr. Golding, (of Withywood) of the gravel.

Captain Simon Booth, of a fwimming in his head, lofs of appetite, &c.—Was eight different times relieved of the above complaints.

* Daniel Hanmer, Efq. of a violent rheumatic complaint in 23 days time.

Thomas Robertfon, of an intermittent fever of 14 months ftanding, by 3 weeks ufe of the water.

Mr. Drower, of a fever and belly-ache in one week.

James Craddock, of the gravel when reduced extremely low. N. B. A great deal of gravel difcharged.

Chriftopher Terry, of the gravel, perfectly recovered in 5 weeks.

William Gordon, (Clarendon) of lownefs of fpirits and depraved appetite.

Mr. Yanckey, (Guanaboa) of ditto.

* Alex. Low, Bricklayer, of the gravel and violent pain in 4 days.

N. B. Thofe marked with an afterifm *, did not ftay long enough to obtain a perfect cure, but were greatly relieved.

CATALOGUE of PLANTS

the moſt remarkable for Uſe or Beauty, which are in the Botanical Garden at Bath.

L Aurus, *Cinnamomum,* The Cinnamon tree
⸺, *Saſſafras,* Saſſafras tree
⸺⸺, *Camphora,* Camphor tree
Garcinia, *Mangoſteena,* Mangoſteen
Mangifera, *Indica,* Mangoe tree
Cycas, *Circinnalis,* Sagoe palm
Mimoſa, *Nilotica,* Gum Arabic tree
Myrica, *Cerifera,* Candleberry myrtle
Croton, *Sebiferum,* E. Ind. Tallow tree
Amygdalus, *Perſica,* Peach tree
⸺⸺, *Communis,* Almond tree
Juniperus, *Bermudienſis,* B. Juniper or cedar
Thuya *Orientalis,* Chineſe Arbor vitæ
Fraxinus, *Ornus,* Manna Aſh
Cupreſſus, *Sempervirens,* Upright Cypreſs
Gardenia, *Florida,* Cape Jeſſamine
Magnolia, *Grandiflora,* Laurel leaf tulip tree
Syringa, *Lilac,* Scotch Lilac tree
Smilax, *Sarſaparilla,* Sarſaparilla
Epidendrum *Vanilla,* Vanilla
Hedyſarum, *Movens,* Moving plant
Hibiſcus, *Roſa Sin ⸺, Ch⸺*

N. B. There are a great many others no lefs ufeful or beautiful, but being more common it was not thought neceffary to enumerate them.

There are alfo feveral curious and unknown Eaft-India plants, prefented by (the never to be forgotten friend of this Ifland) *Lord Rodney,* amongft which is a moft elegant palm, fuppofed to be the walking cane.

F I N I S.

www.ingramcontent.com/pod-product-compliance
Lightning Source LLC
Chambersburg PA
CBHW032110010726
47493CB00008B/2526